CARNIVAL

VIKING

BY
M. C. HELLDORFER
ILLUSTRATED BY
DAN YACCARINO

To Mary and Bill
Celebrating a houseful of grandchildren
—M. C. H.

The artwork was done in alkyds on Bristol paper.

VIKING
Published by the Penguin Group
Penguin Books USA Inc., 375 Hudson Street, New York, New York 10014, U.S.A.
Penguin Books Ltd, 27 Wrights Lane, London W8 5TZ, England
Penguin Books Australia Ltd, Ringwood, Victoria, Australia
Penguin Books Canada Ltd, 10 Alcorn Avenue, Toronto, Ontario, Canada M4V 3B2
Penguin Books (N.Z.) Ltd, 182-190 Wairau Road, Auckland 10, New Zealand

Penguin Books Ltd, Registered Offices: Harmondsworth, Middlesex, England

First published in 1996 by Viking, a division of Penguin Books USA Inc.

1 3 5 7 9 10 8 6 4 2

LIBRARY OF CONGRESS CATALOGING-IN-PUBLICATION DATA
Helldorfer, Mary Claire.
Carnival / by M.C. Helldorfer;
illustrated by Dan Yaccarino.   p.   cm.
Summary : A carnival offers all the fun and excitement of flying balloons,
pitching baseballs, riding ponies, and walking through a haunted house.
ISBN 0-670-86687-3
[1. Carnivals—Fiction. 2. Stories in rhyme.]   I. Yaccarino, Dan, ill. II. Title.
PZ8.3.H413485Car 1996   [E]—dc20   95-34559 CIP AC

Printed in Singapore

Come one, come all!

Tie it

Fly it

Pop it

Toss and

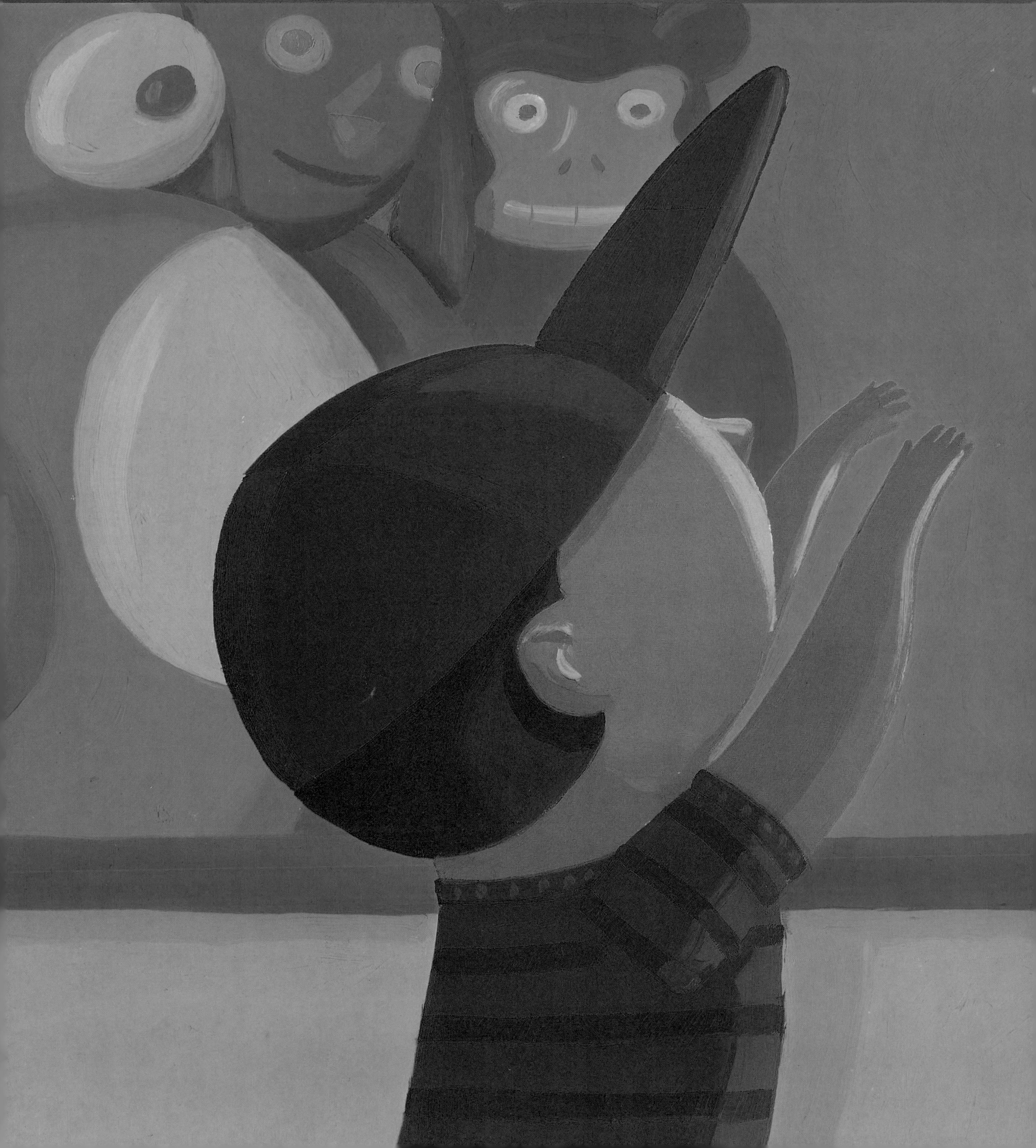

Roll and

toss it

Whack it

Lick it

Crack it

Giddy giddy

giddy-up-it

Munch it

Wish for it

Fish for it

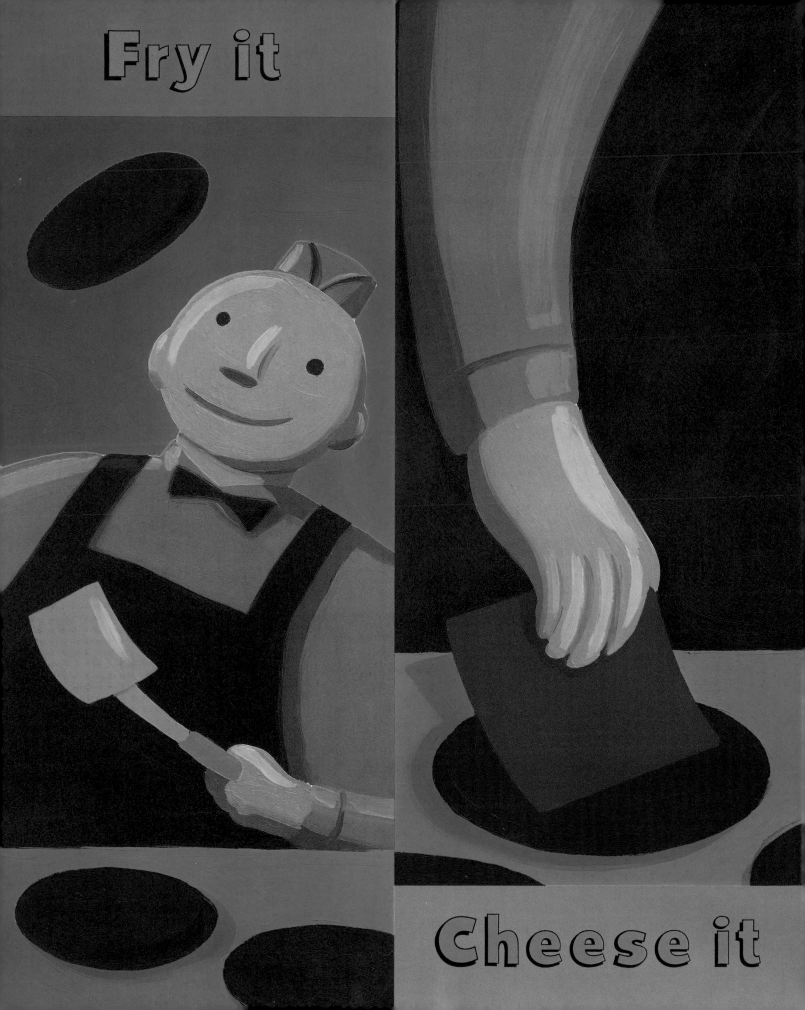

Squeeze it

Whoa!

Shiver quiver

goose bumps oh!

Fly

Toss

Giddy giddy

Whoosh! Bump!

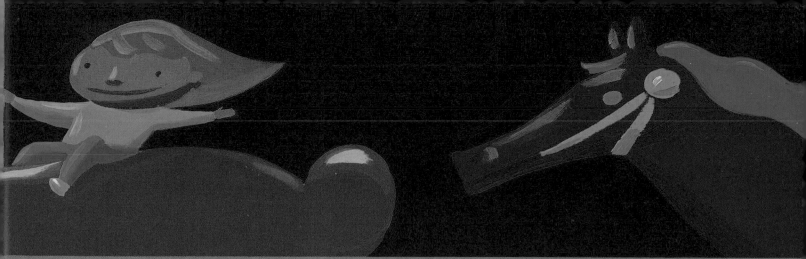

upside-down

Tummy-Oh!

Hey . . .
want to do it again?